The Friendly Creeper Diaries: The Moon City

Book 5: The Secret of the Moon City

Mark Mulle

DEDICATION

This book is dedicated to all Minecraft lovers.

CONTENTS

DAY 8

It was just our luck running into the king. We were cornered. Behind us were skeletons. In front of us were guards and the king himself. Star had fainted from using too much magic. All David and I could do was stare at him.

We had never met the king directly but over the past few months, I had seen paintings of him. He always looked kind in them.

Now, however, the king wasn't looking so kind. He was glaring at us with his arm crossed, wearing a gold cloak over his clothes.

"You're coming with me," He said to us, "The two of you and the girl."

"Are you sure? We were just leaving." David replied.

The king scowled, "Make sure they don't escape."

The guards came over to us. One of them tried to yank Star out of my short arms but I held onto her too tightly. They gave up and instead formed a group around us, pushing us forward after the king.

I glanced at David who only shrugged in return. Fantastic. This was exactly how I thought things were going to go. Having the king take us to the castle again was just the icing on the cake. This time there would be no escape.

As we headed towards the castle, David spoke, "You know, we were just walking around town. Locking us up and tracking us down seems a little over the top."

The king glanced at us over his shoulder, "Don't be a fool. You think I don't see the girl? I'm not blind. I know who she is."

I glanced down at Star. Her eyes were closed and she looked peaceful, as if she was fast asleep in her own bed.

The king went on, "She must have used quite a bit of magic to get you guys out of my dungeon. Her people are fantastic with magic. It is part of the secret of the Moon City. One of the secrets they refused to share for the good of the Over World."

"Oh, so you're trying to tell us they are the bad guys then?" David asked him.

The king stopped walking and turned around to look at us, "This isn't a black and white case about who is bad here."

"That's usually what bad guys say." David replied.

The king narrowed his eyes, "The two of you could have lived quiet lives. You saved us from the Nether. You were able to go back home and live out your life. But no. The two of you are meddling in things you couldn't begin to understand."

Neither David nor myself got to reply. Suddenly, out of the shadows of the rooftops came dark figures swooping down. It almost looked as if they were flying. The dark shapes landed down in the group.

The skeletons lunged, attacking the figures. They looked like Star, in dark cloaks and hoods. They had diamond equipment and began to fight back the skeletons. The king roared for his men to attack.

David and I stood there for a few seconds, unsure what in the world we were supposed to do. Then one of the hooded figures grabbed my arm and turned me around.

"The three of you must come this way."

I couldn't see their face but seeing as they were the ones saving us, I was more likely to go with them than stick around with the king. I nodded and David and I took off after the figure.

It led us down a narrow alleyway. We stopped in front of a wall which looked to be a regular stone wall. But like what Star did back in the dungeon, the figure pressed its hand against it. There was a soft light and then the stone vanished, allowing us a way through.

"Hurry." The figure said as we followed it.

The stone wall appeared behind us, locking us inside. But torches led the way down a winding stone staircase. Star began to stir in my arms.

"Is she going to be okay?" I asked the figure.

"She shouldn't have used so much magic but yes, she will be okay. She needs to rest."

"Thanks for saving us back there." David replied.

"We weren't saving you. We were saving Star." The figure replied.

That made David fall silent. Great, more people that didn't want us. The staircase ended and we were in front of two wide doors. They were also carved out of stone and had carvings in them. In the low lighting, I could see that it was of a dragon flying high in the sky.

The figure pushed the doors open with a groan and then beckoned for us to follow. We trailed after him as Star mumbled in her sleep. My arms were starting to get tired so I hoped she woke up soon.

But the thought of my arms were quickly forgotten when we stepped into the room. Next to me, David let out a gasp. I couldn't help but stare too.

In front of us was the entrance to the Moon City. Made entirely out of stone, there were thick stone pillars holding the ceiling up. There was a large fountain in the middle with fresh water pouring out of a vase at the top. Stars were painted on the ceiling, as if we were under the night sky.

The room widened and I could see city streets ahead of us. Buildings lined the street. Some were in ruins, spilling out onto the street. Others had candle light in the windows, showing that people lived there.

"I can't believe it." David mumbled.

"You were right." I said, surprised.

"I was right." He repeated and even though the king was chasing after us and these people didn't even want us down here, we looked at each other and grinned.

The figure stopped walking when it saw we weren't following. It turned to look at us and lowered its hood. It was an older looking man. He had a beard and his hair was entirely white. His face was made of wrinkles and his skin looked paper thin. He looked ancient. It was surprising how quickly he had been able to move and run.

"I'm Anderson." The man said to us.

We introduced ourselves as he came over and took Star out of my arms. She made a soft noise but still didn't wake up.

"Follow me." Anderson told us.

We glanced at each other quickly before following him into the city. As the street spread out in front of us, we took in the sight. It looked so old. There were markings on some of the homes in a language we didn't know. I could feel people staring at us but we didn't see anyone else.

At the end of the street rose the largest building in this area. Candlelight was pouring out of every window and we could see people moving inside. It seemed to be the busiest area by far. We walked up the crumbling steps toward it.

The doors opened for us and we stepped inside. I was expecting more stone. But the inside of this building was unlike what we had seen so far. Everything was crafted out of objects I hadn't seen in a while. Diamonds were in the floors! There were rubies in the walls! Everything shimmered from the candlelight. The walls were decorated with paintings full of detail showing that same dragon again.

"Wow." I breathed.

Anderson looked at me, "Most of us live here. A few of us live out in the city. But the city has fallen into despair so it is easier to focus on this one building for us to live in."

"Is this a castle?" David asked quietly.

"It used to be, yes. Long ago, we had kings and queens. Now, we just live here without one ruler. Wait here. I have to get Star to our doctor."

"Wait, can't we come with you?" I asked, taking a step forward.

"No. I'm sorry," He paused as if sensing my concern because he then said, "She will be okay."

I nodded, not wanting to push the topic. We weren't even welcome here. Throwing a fit to go with Star wouldn't make things easier for us. Even so, it was difficult watching Anderson leave with her. She had saved and protected us. It was difficult to think that she was hurt at all because of us.

We stood there in the silence and then looked at each other before David went, "What now?"

"No idea. We've seen your precious city. Can we go home now?"

David laughed, "Yeah, somehow I don't think it is that easy anymore."

"Of course not." I replied with a sigh.

We weren't sure if anyone was coming for us or if we were just supposed to sit around here. But it wasn't long before we heard someone coming back. Anderson appeared without Star.

"Originally, Star was told to make sure you two left the city before trouble started. Now, that is too late." He said to us.

David looked bashful but didn't reply.

Anderson went on, "The king will know that we have taken you to the city. He will be furious and will want to find you."

"How has he not found the city after all these years?" I asked curiously.

"Follow me." Anderson said.

So, again, we followed him. We still didn't see anyone as we walked down a beautifully decorated hallway. The amount of wealth around us was mind-blowing. No wonder the king wanted to find the city.

This time we were led into a small dining room. The table was made out of oak and the chairs were crafted perfectly. The food was covered in all sorts of food including richly decorated cakes. Anderson motioned for us to sit down.

"Please, help yourself. You must be hungry." He said.

It was true. We were absolutely starving. Without Anderson having to say twice, we started gobbling up the food. Anderson nibbled on some bread before he started to talk.

"As I'm sure you saw, I gained entrance to the city by changing the blocks in the wall. That sort of magic isn't the regular type of magic that you see in the Over World. It is old magic. A magic that only my people have. Without it, the king cannot ever enter the city."

"So, we wouldn't have been able to either, right?" I ask.

Anderson nods, "Correct. The two of you do not have the magic to gain access to the city. You could follow all the symbols around town and it wouldn't work."

"Why has the king basically sealed off part of the city?" David spoke up.

"He hopes that if people believe that section of the city is cursed, it would be easier to find the Moon City. Empty streets mean anyone walking around in there might know the way to the city. The jewel merchant that you two spoke to works for the king to tell him if anyone is poking around."

"Why don't you guys share the wealth with him? Star said something about the king wanting to have the treasure and knowledge here. She said all the kings have. But there has to be a reason your people won't let the kings come here." I said.

David had a mouthful of cake when he said something. Anderson and I stared at him. He swallowed the cake and laughed.

"Sorry, uhm, what I was trying to say was she made it sound as if there isn't just gold down here."

Anderson nodded but seemed hesitant to tell us more, "That is correct. There is more at stake here than just our wealth. Over the centuries, the kings that have shown interest in our city never had the Over World's best interests at heart. There have been some kings who have left us alone, content to let us handle things ourselves. But for every one king who is okay with us, there are five more who want to wield the power we have down here."

"What is the power?" I asked.

But Anderson didn't reply, instead taking a sip of his water. I got the feeling that we weren't going to be told about what was so powerful here in the Moon City.

David spoke next, "So, what now? If the king knows we are here, like you said, we can't just stroll out and go back home."

"That is correct. You will have to stay here."

We both blinked. Anderson didn't say anything after that. He made it sound as if what he had just said was completely normal.

"Sorry, what?" I finally asked.

"You will have to stay here down with us. You can't go home."

"Sorry, Anderson, that isn't going to work for us. We have lives back home. We can't just stay here." David said.

"You can't leave. The king will go after you."

"So, we'll take care of ourselves. But we can't live here. Surely, you hear how crazy that is, right?" I said.

Anderson put his hands on the table, palm up, as if to say he couldn't do anything about it. All we could do was stare at him. We suddenly didn't feel hungry anymore.

"How about I show you to your rooms and we can discuss it after we all get some sleep?" He finally said.

We nodded because...well, what else were we going to do? By the time we were shown to our rooms, it was extremely late. David's room was across the hall from mine. When the door closed behind me, I heard it softly lock.

Great. Just a nicer dungeon. I tossed my bag on the bed and looked around. The room was just as nicely decorated as the rest of the place. The floor was made of emeralds and the walls had flecks of gold in them. A bed was in the middle of the room. There were no windows. A crafting table was off to one side with a fireplace near it.

I lit up the fireplace because it was chilly and then crawled into bed. Even though I should be exhausted, I found it hard to focus. I wanted to write. So that's what I've been doing. Trying to catch up with everything that has happened. It took me a long time and it is well past midnight.

But what do we do now? Anderson is acting as if we are really going to stay here but there is no way David and I will live down here. We have to –

DAY 9

There was a soft knock on the door that brought me out of my writing. Thinking David had somehow gotten out of his room, I went over to it.

"It's locked," I said after I tried the handle, "How did you get out?"

The door clicked and the handle turned. The door opened but instead of David standing there, it was Star. She was holding a key.

"Clean bill of health." She joked – I hadn't heard her joke before.

"Star, are you okay?" I asked her as she stepped into my room and closed the door behind her.

"Just tired. Really tired. Got a lecture from Anderson about using too much magic. It isn't good for our bodies. But whatever. I'm okay. He told me about wanting you guys to stay down here."

"You understand why we can't, right?" I asked her.

"Yes. I get it."

"Will you help us get out of here?"

Star wandered over to the crafting table and ran her hand along it, lost in thought, "The king will come after you."

"We'll figure it out."

"What if I wanted your help instead?"

"Our help?"

Star turned to look at me, "I was thinking about the two of you. How you wanted to find the city and how it's become more than what you were expecting. But I was thinking about what David said too about us cowering down here, hiding from the king. What if I wanted your help to change that?"

"What would you want to do?"

"I'm going to the council. Anderson is in charge of it."

"He said this place has no real ruler."

"Technically, not one ruler. The council decides what is best for us. I'm going to go with them and tell them what I think we should do. Hopefully, they will agree."

"And if they don't?"

She paused before going, "I don't know. I just think it is time for my people to push back."

"Are you sure? To go against the king - that isn't a small thing."

"I've only ever seen that abandoned part of the city. Imagine being able to really explore. To go wherever I want. I know I have magic and powers that don't exist in the Over World. And I know...I know what my people are protecting down here. But if we expose the king for what he is doing then maybe my people don't have to hide anymore. We can go out there and be free."

"Have you talked to David?"

"No, not yet. I came to you first. I figured David would want to do whatever would lean to the most adventure."

"Yeah, that's pretty accurate." I replied.

"Well?"

"Alright. I mean, you speak to the council first and if they don't help, I guess we will see what we can do. But really think about this, Star."

"Maybe we can escape together. And I can see the world. You understand, don't you?"

I did. Not long ago, my village was completely in secret. No one knew about us and we had very little knowledge of the outside world. What Star wanted was something I had wanted over the years as well.

Even so, I had a hard time believing the council would want to move against the king especially after Anderson told us we would have to live down here. They had lived in hiding for years and years. I doubted they would listen to Star and her pleas to go into the world.

"You should prepare for them to say no. We have to come up with a plan if they don't want to go against the king. Do you have anything like that planned?"

"Sort of." Star said but she didn't add anything to it.

"Alright, well. Get some rest. We won't go anywhere. I'll wait until I hear from you about the council."

She nodded and went to leave the room. Before she left, though, she paused and looked at me.

"Thanks. For carrying me and making sure I got here okay."

"No problem. You saved us enough. I owed you."

She smiled and gave me a small wave before shutting the door behind her. I watched her go and then plopped into bed, completely exhausted. Sleep came for me quickly and I don't even remember anything I may have dreamt up while I slept.

When I woke up, it was because someone was coming into the room. I propped myself up and yawned, rubbing my eyes. I realized it was Star. She was dressed in a blue cloak and her hair was up in a messy bun. Her brown eyes were wide.

"Let me guess...didn't go well?" I asked her, trying to wake up – I wasn't sure how long I had been asleep for.

"No, not at all. They are worried that David and you corrupted me somehow. Twisted my thinking in wanting to go to the surface. I think I did more harm than good."

"Then we need to get out of here," I said, getting up, "The city won't want to go against the king. And the king is going to want to find us down here."

"We can escape but it won't matter."

We turned around to see David shutting my door behind him. When Star asked how he had gotten out of his locked room, he merely wiggled his eyebrows before looking at me.

"What do you mean, it won't matter?" I asked.

"Star's people won't want to fight. And the king wants to fight. That's why nothing has happened all these years. Nothing will change at this point. Star, you can escape but your people will still be forced into hiding. Your people need to see that things can be changed if we all work together. Let Mike and I talk to Anderson."

Star shook her head, "No way."

"Things can't get worse, right? He already wants us stuck down here. Let us talk to him. We can convince him we have to do something here."

Star hesitated and glanced at me before finally nodding her head. Then she told us to wait here.

With Star gone, David looked at me and sighed, "Not sure if Anderson will listen to us but I figured we'd have to try anyway."

"Why do you think Anderson doesn't want to go against the king?"

"Not sure. These people are powerful, Mike. Something here doesn't add up."

It was true. Anderson wanting us stuck down here and his refusal to even consider what Star was saying, as well as telling her perhaps she had been corrupted by us all seemed fishy.

So we sat around and waited….and waited…I wrote in here to catch up. But Star isn't back yet. That can only mean one thing.

DAY 10

"I shouldn't have told her to go back to Anderson," David whispered as we snuck down the hallway, "We should have just taken her and left."

"Yeah, but you did the right thing. Star was talking about escaping on her own and I think she would regret it. As much as she wants to see the outside world, this place is important to her too. If she just left and her people remained trapped under the king's rule, she would feel awful."

We stopped at the end of the hallway and looked around the corner. Torches were along the walls but we didn't see anyone.

"We have no idea where we are going." I pointed out as we walked down this hallway.

"Just try to see if you can hear anything, okay? We can follow voices once we pick some up." David mumbled.

"Do you think Anderson is up to something?" I wondered aloud as we turned down another corner.

"I wouldn't be surprised. What he is up to, though, I don't know. Just something doesn't feel right."

I pulled David back before he turned another corner. We fell silent. I heard voices in the distance. The two of us strained to hear it. It sounded like people were bickering. The hallway was empty. Torches cast long shadows on the floor. But I could see a couple of doors leading to what had to be the council room.

Together, we crept down the hallway. The door was slightly open, making it easier to hear when they were saying.

"This is madness!" A woman was exclaiming, "What is the meaning of this?"

Anderson's voice came next, "This is how things have to be. For too long, we have hidden here in the shadows. For too long, we have allowed the king to rule over us. Whatever the king wanted, we fought against. Why do we do this? You are either with me or against me in this!"

"This is not what Star was suggesting!" Another man exclaimed, "Where did you put the girl?"

"The girl has been corrupted by the surface! Her plan would not work!" Anderson shouted.

"And yours will? Forcing us to go after the king and put you on the throne – that is madness as well!"

David and I glanced at each other silently. That explained Anderson's behavior. He didn't want to find a way to make peace with the king. He wanted to overthrow the king and rule both the Moon City and the Sun City.

"It will never work! No matter how many skeletons you have coming towards us!" Someone cried out.

Skeletons? Suddenly even more concerned, I peeked through the open door to try to see what was going on inside.

Anderson did have tons of skeletons around him. The rest of the council, older people in matching cloaks, were pressed against the opposite wall. I didn't see Star.

"If you listen to me, the skeletons won't need to do anything," Anderson was saying, "Either you help me put myself on the throne and overthrow the king, or you are locked up with Star."

"This is insane," Someone said, "Even for you. I thought we all agreed we had to stay down here. What we have down here cannot fall into the hands of some king – that includes you!"

I turned my head to tell David we had to do something – but like always, David wasn't one for planning. He pushed past me into the room. I knew he had no plan. But lately he was more of a 'think later' sort of person. With a groan, all I could do was follow him into the room.

Anderson whirled around and stared at us, "What are you two doing here?"

"We didn't really feel like living here," I replied, "So, we went for a walk."

He narrowed his eyes at us, "You're going back to your rooms."

"And what, let you overthrow the king? You don't sound much better than the king, honestly." David snapped.

"You're going to let these people go. And you're going to tell us where Star is." I demanded.

At this, Anderson laughed, "Or what?"

Well, he got us there. We couldn't actually really do a thing but it had been worth a shot. We shrugged in unison.

"Get them!" He yelled at his skeletons.

The skeletons lunged after us. At the same time, the rest of the council took this chance to strike back at Anderson. I rolled forward as a skeleton brought its sword down. Then I grabbed its bony hand and yanked the sword out of its hand.

I looked down at it. It was made of gold. It was a pretty sword but gold was a weak metal for crafting. Either Anderson didn't know or he wanted his swords to look pretty so much that he didn't care it wasn't the best things to use in combat.

Next to me, David had also managed to grab a sword and also a shield. As a skeleton jumped out at me, our swords clashed together. The metal made a soft ringing noise. I pressed my strength against the skeleton's gold sword – and it snapped. If the skeleton had actually had a face, it would have looked surprised. Then I swung my own sword and it turned to ash in front of me.

"Where is Anderson?" I cried out to David as he took down a skeleton.

"Ran off in this mess!"

"We have to find Star!" I exclaimed as I yanked a shield out of a pile of skeleton ash.

A skeleton threw its sword at me out of an act of desperation. I brought my shield up and it bounced off of it although it dented the gold. Behind the skeleton, one of the council members turned it to ash with magic.

The skeletons were quickly losing the battle. Between us fighting them and the council members with their magic, soon there was nothing left. One of the members came up to me, out of breath.

She was an older woman with a head full of grey hair, "Star is down in the prison below. Here is the key," She handed it to me; "you go get her. We will go after Anderson."

"Where did he go?" David asked.

"It appears just now that he's been planning this for a long time. He has creatures at his disposal, ready to attack. He wants to launch a full attack on the king and put himself on the throne using our deepest secret." The woman said.

"What is that?" I asked.

But the council didn't reply. Whatever this secret was, it wasn't our place to learn it yet.

The woman went on, "My name is Grace. I'm Anderson's sister."

"Bad stroke of luck." David grumbled behind me but Grace ignored him.

"I had no idea he was planning this. He never, ever spoke about going to the surface. But if he wants to expose our people, use our powers, and overthrow the king, we cannot allow that. My brother is not fit to be a king. Whatever ideas he has, they are rooted in darkness."

"He wouldn't be better than the king in the Over World?"

"No. No, the king above us – he wants our power down here too. But my brother is no better. They are both sides of the same coin. We have to save the Moon City from Anderson and the king."

"Wonderful. Things just keep getting worse." I mumbled, glancing at David, who shrugged.

"Alright, we'll go get Star." David said.

"She was brave, coming to him to try to convince him to have a peaceful resolution for the king. I agreed with her and sided with her. Anderson did not like that. He didn't want to co-exist with the Over World. He wants to rule it."

"Of course he does," I said, "We always seem to run into guys like this."

Grace looked confused but David laughed before pulling on my arm. Grace shouted directions after us and a warning to look out for skeletons and then we were back in the hallway.

"Do you still regret coming along?" David asked me.

"Ask me when we see how this turns out." I joked and then we set off to find Star.

Grace had told us directions but the building we were in really felt like a beautifully done up castle. We got lost twice before we managed to find the staircase we needed to head down. Torches lined the spiral staircase and I could see more carvings on the stone here.

"Wonderful, another dungeon." David grumbled as we headed down it.

"I wish we had stronger weapons. These gold ones aren't that great."

"Just proves Anderson doesn't know what he is doing," David replied, "Gold swords and shields are nice for decorations. But giving them to your skeleton army? Even an iron sword could destroy it."

"Well, we can use that to our advantage, I guess. If we ever find stronger weapons."

The prison entrance was in front of us. Through the bars, we could see more skeletons. They were marching around, as if Star needed that much protection. On second thought, it was us coming to her rescue so maybe they did need this much protection.

"Ready?" I asked David.

He nodded. Together, we kicked open the barred door and ran inside. The skeletons turned and attacked us on sight. The quarters were close and tight, making combat difficult. I took one skeleton down only to have another right on my heels. I spun around and lifted up my shield, barely blocking the attack.

Star threw herself against the bars of her cell, "My magic is blocked! Whatever Anderson did to me when I ran out of magic, it wasn't healing me!

I kicked one of the skeletons back and tossed her the key. It landed just outside the cell. Star tried to grab it but it was just out of her reach. Meanwhile, David was backed into a corner by two skeletons.

I ran over and knocked one against the wall, spinning and raising my shield to block another blow from the second skeleton. Then David brought his sword down and turned the skeleton to ash. The other skeleton was getting to his feet. I took care of it.

The dungeon was empty. David picked up the key since Star couldn't grab it and unlocked her cell door. She practically toppled out of it.

Speaking quickly, she said, "Anderson didn't heal me when I came to him. He must have given me something to mute my magic. It hasn't come back yet. I won't be of much help."

"Yes you will," David replied, "You know the layout of the city and we don't."

"Anderson is planning –"

"We know," I cut her off because we were low on time, "Grace told us."

"You saw Grace? Is everyone else okay?"

"Yeah, they're going to try to stop Anderson."

Star shook her head, "I was so stupid. I went back to him because I thought he would listen. I thought maybe if I could just convince him to talk to you two…"

"Don't blame yourself. Grace said that it appears that Anderson had this planned for a long time, way before we got involved." I said, hoping to comfort her.

She smiled weakly, "That's good, I guess. Although…not really. This whole thing is a mess. Convincing the king we were on his side and could work together was one thing. But now Anderson has a skeleton army and our power behind him – he basically wants to force himself on the throne."

David wiped some sweat off his brow, "Are you going to tell us yet what the big secret is? What the thing is that your people guard down here? The power or whatever?"

Star fell silent. Even now, it seemed we weren't going to learn that information. It was probably from years of having to hide it. It was hard to break out of that routine. Believe me, I knew.

"What's the next step?" I asked her instead.

"I think I know where he is going. But the council will move too slowly. We should go."

She turned to walk out of the prison. David and I hurried after her.

"What do you mean, they will move too slowly?" I asked.

"They're going to stand around and fight about what to do. Grace will want them to hurry but they won't hurry enough. I know where our power is. I can take us there."

David grabbed her arm and she stopped to look at him as he asked, "You aren't supposed to know where it is, are you?"

A sheepish look crossed her face, "No. No, only the council is supposed to know the exact location of where to go."

"How do you then?" I asked curiously.

"I followed the council one time. Hey, don't look at me like that! I was young, okay? I was curious."

"Doesn't matter. Works in our favor. Lead the way."

"We need magic to access it. If my magic doesn't come back..."

"Don't worry about that now," I put a comforting hand on her shoulder, "We will deal with it if it happens."

She nodded and then we headed towards the staircase. It was blocked, however, by a wither skeleton. When it saw us, it gestured at its sword, signaling it was going to attack. Star stumbled back. Without her magic, there wasn't much she could do in a fight.

The wither skeleton made a strange clacking noise with its jaw and ran towards us. I had almost forgotten how quickly the wither skeletons could run – almost. I pushed Star out of the way and rolled to the side as its golden sword crashed against the stones.

David spun around its back and slashed at it with his sword. The wither skeleton swung his arm behind him and sent David flying backwards. He slammed against the wall and landed at the base of the stairs.

Star called his name and ran over to him, making sure he was okay. I ran forward and slammed my shield against the wither skeleton, throwing him off balance. It was unsteady on its feet as I brought my sword down.

But our swords met and suddenly mine snapped in half. The gold had apparently had enough. The pieces clattered to the floor and all I could see was the gold of the wither skeleton's sword about to hit me.

Then Star slammed into the wither skeleton. Together, they tumbled to the floor. It dropped its own sword and I snatched it up. The wither skeleton tossed Star off of it as it got to its feet.

But this time, I had the upper hand. I attacked and the wither skeleton turned to ash in front of my eyes.

"Everyone okay?" I asked.

Star was wincing as she got to her feet, "Yeah, never better."

David was sitting up now, rubbing his ankle, "Think I sprained this."

"Can you walk?"

"Yeah, but I will slow you down." He said as I helped him to his feet.

Star hurried over and helped him up as well. David let out a grunt of pain and shook his head.

"You guys should go ahead."

"What?" I exclaimed, "We can't leave you behind."

"I'll only slow you down, Mike. Star knows where to go. You have to go with her."

"What will you do?" I asked him.

"I'll go back to the council. I'll try to tell them to hurry up."

"I hate that you have to go," Star said, "But that might be for the best. We have to move quickly. And if you are there talking to the council, you can work with Grace. Maybe they will stop fighting about what to do and realize they have to stop Anderson."

David nodded, "I'll do that then."

"I don't like this." I said.

"I'll be okay. We've been split up before, remember?" He said to me.

I did remember, back in the Nether, for those moments where David had been locked up by Lucas. I knew that he was right. We did have to move quickly. I nodded and then we began to walk back up the stairs.

David's progress was slow. He had injured his ankle and it showed. He was limping but pretending it was fine. When we were finally back out in the hallway, he looked at us.

"Go on ahead. I'll be okay, promise. I'm just going to be with Grace."

"Be careful either way." I said to him.

He nodded and then with one last look, he limped down the hallway. Star looked at me. Her skin was pale and she looked nervous. I hoped that whatever Anderson had done to her hadn't ruined her magic. If it did, what would stop Anderson from doing it to everyone down here? That would give him the upper hand.

"Come on," She said to me, "We have to hurry."

I nodded and we took off at a run. I was expecting us to go straight ahead but we took a staircase up a level.

"Why are we going up?" I asked her as we ran.

"Shortcut." She said over her shoulder.

She stopped in front of a closed door and opened it, sticking her head inside. Then she told me to follow her. The room was filled with books. Most of them looked ancient and in a language I didn't understand. The room faintly musty from the smell of them.

But Star didn't bother to look at any of the books. Instead, she crossed over to the other side of the room where there was a window. She opened that up and peered up and then looked at me.

"We have to climb up. Are you a good climber?"

"I'm okay. It'd be better if we had pickaxes."

"Well, we don't. We will have to make the best of it."

"This is the shortcut?"

"Yeah. Come on!" She urged me.

With a sigh, I followed her out the window. I was a decent climber but Star, who was used to running around rooftops and jumping around, scaled the side of the building with ease. She looked a bit like a monkey scampering after a banana with how quickly she moved.

I was a bit slower. I made the mistake of looking down once, curious to see what was below. We weren't up that high – probably only about three stories. But down below, instead of the city, was just darkness. It looked like a hole that lead to the center of the earth.

"Uh, Star? What is down there, anyway?" I called up to her.

"Nothing good!" She called back – not a clear answer but it told me all I needed to know about accidentally falling, "The city is on the edge of this hole. We think the city used to be larger but over the years, it just fell apart!"

"Wonderful!" I exclaimed.

Star got to the rooftop first and helped pull me over. I landed with a thud and got to my feet quickly. The city was below us and for the first time I got a good look at it. I imagined that it was beautiful once. But the years hadn't been kind to it. As grand as it looked, many sections had fallen apart and I could see just how old it was.

Star had taken off at a jog across the roof of the building, which was slanted and made it hard to walk across. She pointed to a building nearby. The roof looked as if it was in disrepair.

"Going to jump over there, alright?"

"Yeah, looks completely safe." I replied.

"Wait, do you see that?" Star pointed.

29

I strained my eyes but I saw it. In the distance, it looked like flames. Torches, maybe. A group of people were marching with them.

"Must be Anderson and his skeleton army."

She was right. On a closer look, I could see that it wasn't people holding the torch but things. Skeletons with weapons.

"We're running out of time." I said.

She nodded and then took off at a run. Then she leapt into the air. For a couple of dreadful seconds, I was afraid Star was going to fall. But she landed on the roof perfectly and turned to look at me.

"Come on!" She gestured for me to follow.

Wow, I really did not want to follow her. I will be honest. The roof looked as if it could fall apart at any moment. Knowing my luck, it would. But I knew that I had to do this. Shoving my fear to the side, I held my breath, ran and jumped.

For a few seconds, it felt as if I was flying. Then I was crashing. I landed on the roof hard at an awkward angle.

And what I had feared completely happened.

The roof groaned under my impact. After having Star jump on it, and then me, it proved to be too much. It snapped and then we were falling. Star let out a yelp of surprise as the roof gave way. We toppled through the ruined building and landed on the second floor.

I groaned and rolled on my back. Star sat up quickly, rubbing her arms and checking for injuries. The wooden floor beneath us groaned as if that was going to snap too.

"Get up, get up. We have to hurry. The skeletons will have heard that for sure."

Quickly, I got to my feet. Star yanked me forward as the wood creaked underneath our every step. She swung her legs outside the window and pushed off the ledge, jumping to the next house. She landed against the roof and grabbed the edge, pulling herself over.

It was an amazing jump. It was a jump that a skilled person could do after years of climbing and jumping around.

Myself? Not so much. I wasn't exactly feeling very confident. But the floor cracked loudly beneath my feet and I knew I had no choice. I grabbed the edges of the window frame and hoped for better luck the second time.

I pushed off and leapt through the air. I stuck my hands out to grab the roof. They grabbed the wooden frame but there was a snapping noise and then I was toppling down. The ground seemed to rise up to meet me. I stuck out my hands and grabbed onto a window frame that luckily held. I slammed against the wall and gasped in surprise.

Above me, Star looked down, "Are you okay?"

"Never better!" I said, straining.

"Climb through the window and meet me on the roof!" She called down.

Wonderful. I managed to pull myself through the window and landed on the floor. I hoped that the floor wouldn't fall apart. Luckily, this floor was made out of stone and didn't give on me. I got to my feet and found a ladder leading to the roof.

I climbed up it and pushed open the door. Star's worried face appeared in front of me.

"Mike, they've found us. We have to go faster."

"Even better." I joked as I got to the roof.

Skeletons had indeed found us. They had climbed on a roof a little bit away from us and were firing arrows. I put up my shield to try to block our heads as we went to the edge of the roof.

"One more jump. Think you can make it? I didn't realize you were such a bad jumper."

"Thanks," I replied and then nodded, "I don't really have a choice, do I?"

"Yeah, that's true."

An arrow slammed into my shield and dented it. Man, I didn't like gold equipment. Ahead of us were the ruins of what was probably a large house at one point. Dragons were carved in the walls and there was a broken sign hanging off of it. It might have been an inn at some point.

"We jump on the roof and we're going to cut through the building, okay? In case we get lost, there is a fountain at the other side we need to go to."

"Alright. Be careful."

"Thanks. Don't muck it up, okay?" Star said to me and then she was running at full speed.

It almost looked as if she was flying. She leapt across the gap from our building to the inn with ease. Arrows flew by her as if they couldn't touch her. Then Star landed on her feet on the roof and ducked behind the chimney to block the arrows from getting to her.

My turn. I lowered my shield and then tossed it off the building. It was dented and was about to break anyway. I ran as fast as I could go and pushed off with the balls of my feet like I had seen Star do.

Then I was soaring through the air. I was waving my arms around wildly as if I could fly. An arrow barely missed me as I crashed painfully into the roof. I skidded along it until Star grabbed me. I probably would have kept going if she hadn't grabbed me.

"You made it! Come on!"

No time to catch my breath or be relieved. I got to my feet and Star opened the door on the roof to the next floor. We jumped down and landed into the hallway. Yes, I had been right. At one point this had been an inn. We ran past a bunch of ruined bedrooms and were about to barrel down the stairs when Star stopped.

I practically crashed into her back and looked over her to see why she had stopped running. Skeletons were at the bottom of the staircase, all armed and waiting for us. Star stuck out her hands but shook her head.

"My magic is still gone." She said desperately.

"Hold back." I said and charged the group.

They had iron swords. I knew my gold one was going to break. But I didn't mind. The fact they had iron swords was a blessing. Either Anderson had only given certain skeletons gold ones – maybe ones he thought were important – or he had realized how weak gold swords were.

In any case, I swung my sword at the first skeleton. It took a step backwards and smacked into a second skeleton which lost its footing and fell. A third skeleton slashed at me with its sword. My gold sword met his iron one – and quickly snapped in half.

The skeleton looked almost surprised by this. I took advantage of this and pushed forward, causing the skeleton to trip.

I grab its bony arm and yanked the iron sword free and then spun around, attacking it with all my strength. The skeleton turned to ash, leaving me with the two others. The first skeleton brought its shield up when I lunged and struck. The second skeleton was circling around me.

Star came running down the stairs. She was holding something but I couldn't tell what it was. She flung it at the second skeleton's head and it shattered. It was a glass bottle. The shattering distracted it and gave me an opening.

I brought my sword down and kicked the skeleton back. It fell against an old marble countertop. Behind me, Star kept throwing glass bottles at the other skeleton, distracting it. I finished off the skeleton, watched it turn to ash and then turned around to focus on the final skeleton.

One glass bottle banged against its head and I struck. The skeleton was too thrown off to attack. Once it was ash at my feet, I looked at Star.

"Good thinking." I said to her.

She came down the stairs and picked up one of the skeleton's iron swords and went, "I can't really fight. But this will have to do until my magic returns."

"Alright, let's go." I said and we walked down the second staircase to the main floor.

We were halfway down the stairs when all of a sudden, there was a loud explosion. The building shook around us and I went flying down the stairs. I landed at the bottom as Star landed on my back.

The building shuddered violently as another explosion tore through it. The building was being blown up! Anderson must have known we were inside and were telling the skeletons just to bring the entire building down around us.

Star scampered to her feet and grabbed me, pulling me up. She told me to run. I took off as fast I could as the floor above us began to crack. Pieces of the building were falling down around us. I could see the exit – would I make it in time?

There was a third explosion and the second floor above us suddenly gave out. I rolled underneath a hollow metal countertop as everything crashed down around us. The marble groaned as if it was going to snap too.

After a few moments, everything went still. I let out a breath that I had been holding and looked around. I had been lucky in finding this place to hide. What about Star?

I called her name but there was no answer. Where had Star said to meet if we had gotten separated? A fountain, right?

I rolled out of the hiding spot and pushed the stones that had fallen out of the way. I was worried that I was stuck beneath a lot of rocks but in a stroke of good luck, I managed to push my way through in a few minutes.

I popped out and looked around the wreckage. The back of the building, where I had been, had been completely destroyed. The front of it, however, was vaguely still upright. It looked as if it was slanting from the explosion.

I didn't see Star. When the building had exploded, I had been ahead of her. There was a chance that she was in the front of the building and we had gotten separated.

In any case, I had a few seconds before Anderson's skeleton group realized I was okay. I had to take Star's advice and meet her at the fountain. Hopefully, she would make it there.

I took off straight ahead, stumbling over the wreckage. My ears were still ringing from the sound of it and it threw me off a little. Even so, I rounded the corner and saw the fountain in front of me.

I made myself run. I looked behind me to make sure that I wasn't being followed. There were no skeletons. That was good because my hearing was still not all there. I turned the corner and saw the fountain in front of me.

It was of a creeper which was surprising. I wanted to ask Star why there was a fountain of a creeper in the middle of this old city...but she wasn't there. I walked in a circle and whispered her name but no one appeared.

Maybe she was in the wreckage and I should have stayed. I am about to turn around to find her when she comes out of a side alleyway. She says something to me but I point to my ears and shrug.

Star comes over and says close to my face, "Are you okay?"

"Yes, besides my hearing. I was worried you got stuck."

"No. It came close but you were a few steps ahead of me and got it harder than I did. My hearing took a hit too. So stay close to me, okay?"

I nodded and pointed to the fountain, "Why do you have a creeper fountain in your city?"

Star looked up at it, "Oh, that. I actually don't know. A lot of our ancient history has been lost to us through the years. I have no idea why we have a creeper statue here."

"That's weird. Never seen a creeper statue before."

"Wouldn't it be funny if your people and my people once used to help each other?"

"Extremely." I said and then she went over to the edge of the fountain.

"Alright. Here goes nothing."

She stuck out her hand at the fountain…and nothing happened. She mumbled something under her breath and dropped her hand.

"My magic is still cut off. It feels as if there is a block or something there."

"You need magic now?"

"Yeah, the way in is under this fountain. But only my magic can open it."

I was about to tell her to try it again when skeletons came around a corner. We both hadn't heard them because of our poor hearing. Star looked alarmed. I raised my sword.

"Star! I'll hold them off but you have to try your hardest to get past the magic barrier, okay?"

"It might not work!" She said, panicked.

"Well, try!"

She nodded and stuck out her hands. The first skeleton came to me and I threw myself into the battle. I had to keep the skeletons off of Star. She had to be able to get past the barrier on her magic or we were going to be in serious trouble. Whatever Anderson did to her had to wear off sometime, didn't it?

I took down two skeletons and spun around, snatching up a shield that one had dropped. I picked it up just in time because I managed to deflect a blow from another sword.

But no matter how many I took down, the skeletons still seemed to keep coming. A squad of them appeared on a roof top with arrows.

"Uh, Star?! I need you to hurry!" I cried out to her as the skeletons became almost overwhelming.

"Mike, I don't think it is going to work!"

My back pressed against Star as the skeleton closed in and I yelled, "It needs to, Star!"

With a panicked scream, she raised her hands up to the sky. Then there was a booming noise. For a worried second, I thought that perhaps there was another explosion about to go off.

But no, whatever thing that had been holding Star back finally wore off. Lighting rained down around us, striking the skeletons and turning them to ash. In seconds, every one of them had turned into a small ash pile.

When it was over, Star leaned against the fountain, catching her breath. I looked around to make sure no more skeletons were coming and then turned to look at her.

"Are you okay?"

She nodded, "Yeah, just…crazy amount of power there. I broke through the barrier. Whatever Anderson did to me wore off just in time."

"Are you sure you're okay?"

"Yeah. I'll let you know if I feel weak from using too much magic." She said and then turned to look at the fountain.

She pressed her hand against it and the creeper glowed a bright green. For a few seconds, it shone brightly before turning back to grey.

Then the stones in front of the statue vanished completely, showing a staircase.

"Guess we are going down this creepy staircase?" I asked.

She nodded and went first. I followed after her. The stones appeared behind me. Torches lit the way as we walked down the steps. The middle of the steps was slanted from years of people walking down here.

The staircase went on for what felt like forever. Star didn't say anything. It was clear that she had gone this way before and knew where we were heading. I hoped that we were ahead of the pack.

Had David gotten to Grace? Had he told them to hurry up? Had Anderson managed to find out we were ahead of him in getting to whatever this secret was? These were all questions I did not have the answer to.

All I could do was follow Star. We finally got to the end of the staircase. We were in a very long stone hallway. I could hear water dripping somewhere in the distance. I ran my fingers along the walls, over carvings.

"What is the story behind these carvings?"

"How my people formed this city. Why we stay hidden." Star said as she walked by them without looking.

"Why isn't everyone in your city allowed down here?"

"Just the council is. We are worried if too many people know what is down here, they might get ideas to rebel. Go to the surface."

"Well, the council only plan really worked out for everyone." I joked as we got to the end of the hallway.

"True. Probably should change that rule."

"Why did you follow them?"

"I was too curious. I just wanted to know what was going on. I had to know."

"You can get us through these doors?"

Star nodded and pressed both her hands against the door. The door reacted instantly to her touch and glowed a bright green. Then the doors opened slowly, grinding loudly open.

Beyond it was darkness. Star stepped inside the room. Even though it was dark, I could hear something breathing inside. I suddenly felt afraid. But Star didn't look bothered. She didn't look afraid at all. So I followed her in.

As soon as her feet touched the ground in this room, it also reacted to her. Torches began to light up the area. We were in a dome shaped room with a high ceiling. Jewels littered the room. At first, I thought that was what the secret was – lots of jewels.

But then, I realized the jewels were moving. Something was breathing. Then I saw two eyes. They opened slowly and saw the two of us. The creature yawned, opening its giant mouth.

"That's a dragon." I breathed as the creature stood up.

Then I noticed the jewels were part of its skin. It was covered in jewels and gems and glittered underneath the torches.

Star looked at me over her shoulder, "This is our secret. This is what we have to hide. The Moon Dragon."

Then she fell silent and turned back to look at the massive dragon. It had gotten to its feet now. It was waking up and looked eager to see us.

I should have been afraid. Yet all I could think was how much we had to stop Anderson from freeing this creature onto the Over World.

ABOUT THE AUTHOR

Mark Mulle is a passionate Minecraft gamer who writes game guides, short stories, and novels about the Minecraft universe. He has been exploring, building, and fighting in the game ever since its launch, and he often uses in-game experiences for inspiration on creating the best fiction for fellow fans of the game. He works as a professional writer and splits his time between gaming, reading, and storytelling, three hobbies and lifelong passions that he attributes to a love of roleplaying, a pursuit of challenging new perspectives, and a visceral enjoyment the vast worlds that imagination has to offer. His favorite thing to do, after a long day of creating worlds both on and off the online gaming community, is to relax with his dog, Herobrine, and to unwind with a good book. His favorite authors include Stephen King, Richard A. Knaak, George R. R. Martin, and R. A. Salvatore, whose fantasy works he grew up reading or is currently reading. Just like in Minecraft, Mark always strives to level up, so to speak, so that he can improve his skills and continue to surprise his audience. He prefers to play massive multiplayer online games but often spends time in those games fighting monsters one on one and going solo against the toughest mobs and bosses he can manage to topple. In every game, his signature character build is a male who focuses mostly on crafting weapons and enchanting, and in every battle, he always brings a one hander sword and a shield with as much magical attributes as he can pour into them. Because he always plays alone, he likes to use his game guides to share all the secrets and knowledge he gains, and who know—he may have snuck some information into his fiction as well. Keep an eye out for his next book!

Disclaimer
This is a work of fiction. Names, characters, businesses, places, events and incidents are either the products of the author's imagination or used in fictitious manner. Any resemblance to actual persons, living or dead, or actual events is purely coincidental.

Author's Note: This short story is for your reading pleasure. The characters in this "Minecraft Adventure Series" such as Steve, Endermen or Herobrine...etc. are based on the Minecraft Game coming from Minecraft ®/TM & © 2009-2013 Mojang / Notch

CPSIA information can be obtained
at www.ICGtesting.com
Printed in the USA
LVOW13s1954220217
525093LV00010B/1128/P